THE SUBSIDIARY

MATÍAS CELEDÓN

THE SUBSIDIARY

TRANSLATED FROM
THE SPANISH BY
SAMUEL RUTTER

MELVILLE HOUSE
BROOKLYN · LONDON

THE SUBSIDIARY

First published by Alquimia Ediciones as *La Filial*
Copyright © 2012 by Matías Celedón
Translation copyright © 2016 by Melville House Publishing, LLC
First Melville House printing: August 2016

Melville House Publishing   8 Blackstock Mews
46 John Street   and   Islington
Brooklyn, NY 11201   London N4 2BT

mhpbooks.com   facebook.com/mhpbooks   @melvillehouse

Library of Congress Cataloging-in-Publication Data
Names: Celedón Pinto, Matías, 1981– author. | Rutter, Samuel, translator.
Title: The subsidiary / Matias Celedon ; translated from the Spanish by
     Samuel Rutter.
Other titles: Filial. English
Description: First edition. | Brooklyn, NY : Melville House, 2016. | First
     published in Spanish as La filial (Santiago : Alquimia, 2012). |
     Description based on print version record and CIP data provided by
     publisher; resource not viewed.
Identifiers: LCCN 2016019137 (print) | LCCN 2016008333 (ebook) |
     ISBN 9781612195452 (ebook) | ISBN 9781612195445 (hardback)
Subjects: LCSH: Corporations—Employees—Fiction. | Subsidiary
     corporations—Fiction. | Psychological fiction. | Experimental fiction. |
     BISAC: FICTION / Political.
Classification: LCC PQ8098.413.E45 (print) | LCC PQ8098.413.E45
     F5513 2016 (ebook) | DDC 863/.7—dc23
LC record available at https://lccn.loc.gov/2016019137

Design by Marina Drukman

Printed in China
1   3   5   7   9   10   8   6   4   2

THE SUBSIDIARY

TO ALL PERSONNEL.

POWER SUPPLY
WILL BE INTERRUPTED BETWEEN
08:30 AND 20:00.

ALL PERSONNEL MUST
REMAIN AT
THEIR WORKSTATIONS.

THE SUBSIDIARY takes
NO RESPONSIBILITY FOR
DAMAGE OR THEFT
WITHIN THE PREMISES.

ATTENTION:

FIRST OUTAGE

I INTERRUPT MY DAILY
TASKS TO MAKE
A RECORD.

THE POWER IS OUT.

THEY HAVE CLOSED OFF THE EXITS.

THE PHONE LINES
ARE DOWN.

SHOUTS CAN BE HEARD OUTSIDE.

THEY HAVE LEFT US ALONE.

05 JUN 2008

THERE IS STILL
ENOUGH LIGHT
IN THE SHADOWS
TO WRITE BY.

I AM ABLE TO DISTINGUISH
THE LETTERS FROM THE DUST.

THROUGH THE
SHARP SLATS OF A
BLIND.

SOME LIGHT,
A FINE WHITE NEEDLE.

A FLY
CROSSES THE THRESHOLD
OF DUST.

IT DISAPPEARS.

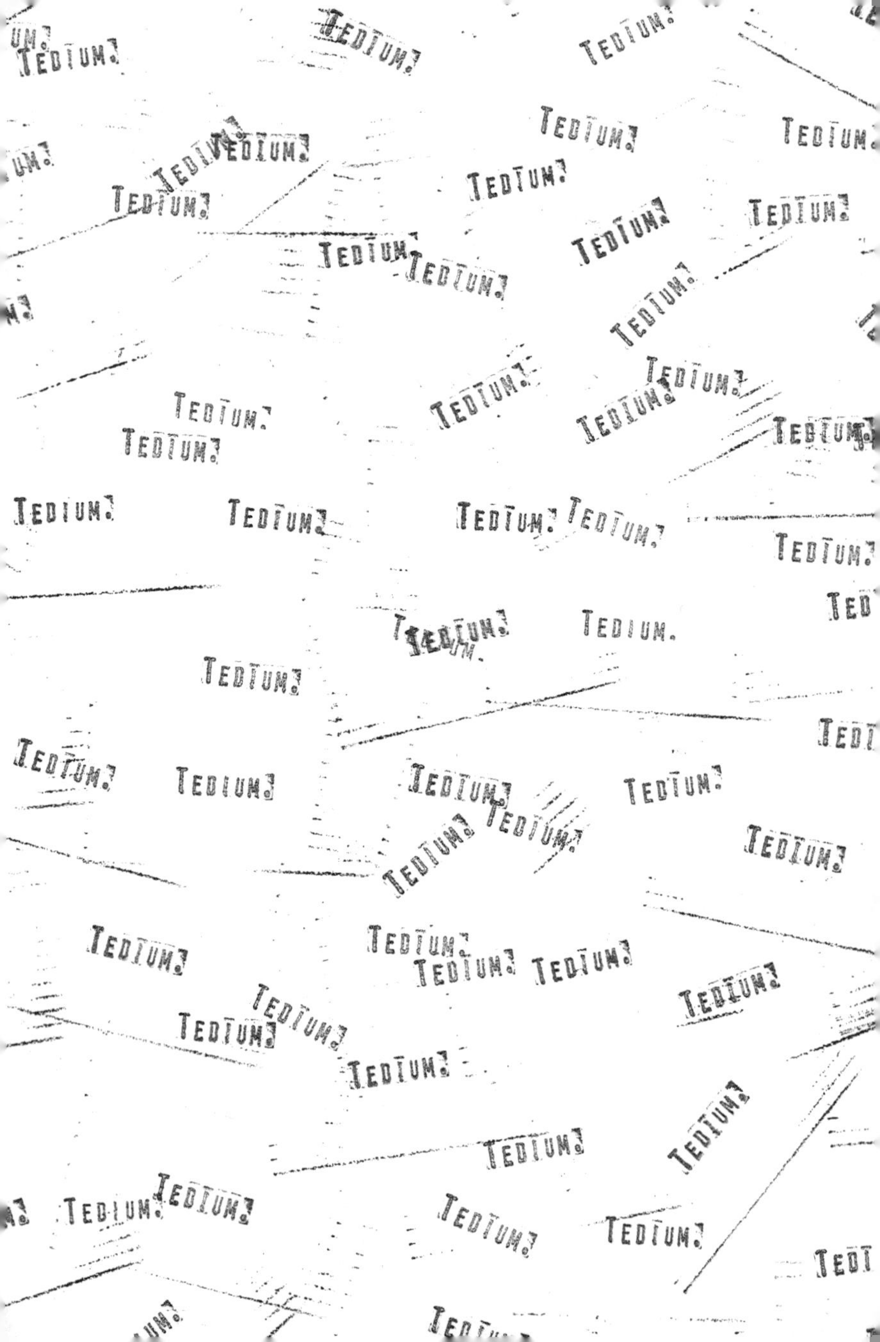
TEDIUM.

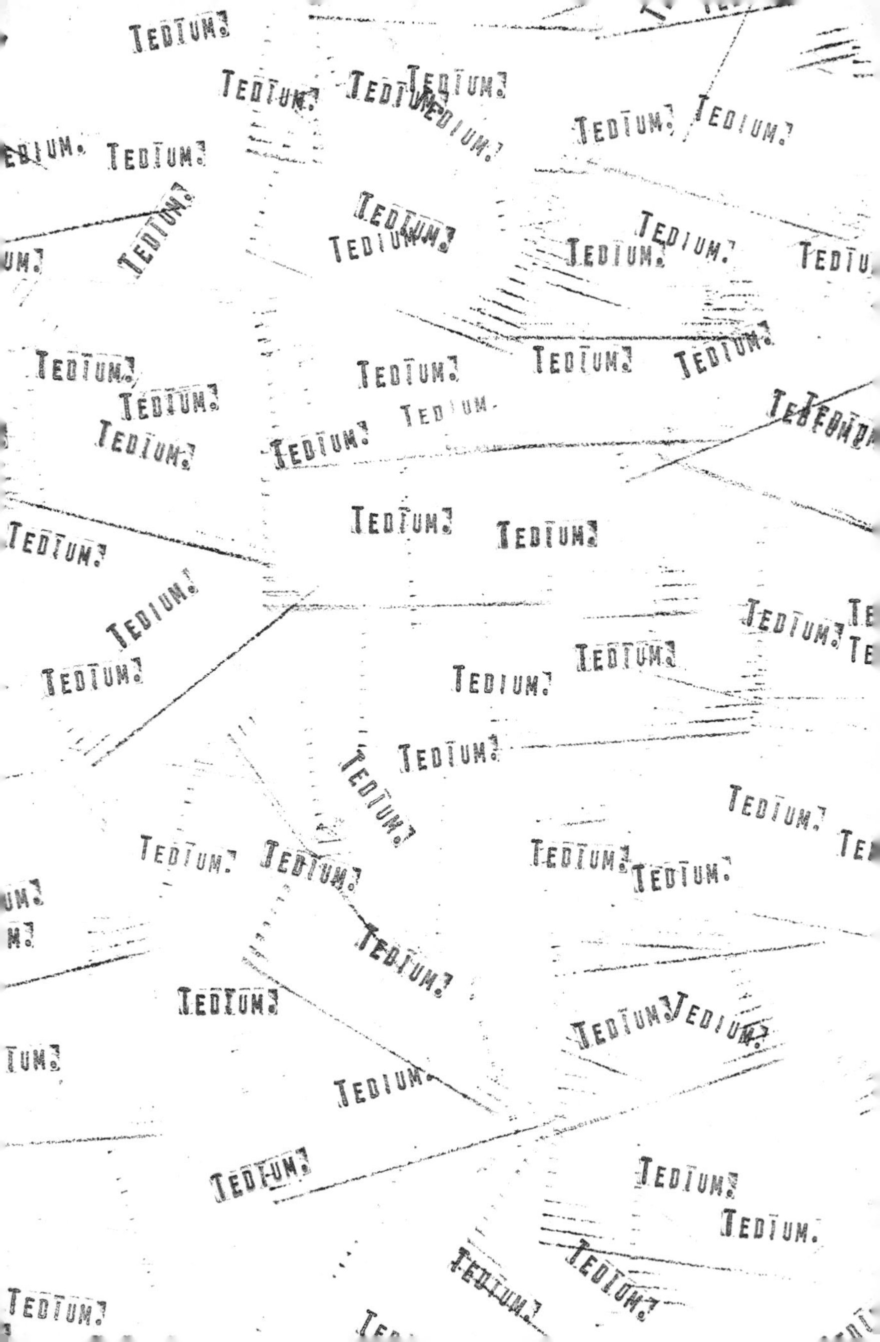
TEDIUM.

A DEAD FLY.

06 JUN 2008

THE DEAF GIRL GETS UP
FROM HER SEAT AND
ASKS ME:

"WHAT DO YOU DO?"

"I SAVE PEOPLE."

THE SUBSIDIARY

INTERNAL
RESIDENT

SENTENCING OFFICE
(013-RTNL.ACRMPTS)

THE DEAF GIRL
ASKS AGAIN:
"WHAT'S YOUR JOB?"

"I STAMP THE ORDERS,
THE INSTRUCTIONS, THE
MANDATES-"

THE DEAF GIRL INTERRUPTS ME.

She asks:

"Aren't there any candles?"

SHE READS MY LIPS,
BUT IT'S DARK.

SHE TOUCHES ME,
LIKE THE BLIND GIRL
IN THE ELEVATOR.

MEASURE
OVERTURNED

I ASK HER:
   "WANT TO FUCK?"

"GIVE ME A CANDLE," SHE SAYS.

THE DEAF GIRL INSISTS.

APPROVED

I PULL DOWN HER SKIRT.

SHE SWALLOWS.

SHE BECOMES FRIGHTENED.

SHE HEARS HERSELF!

THE DEAF GIRL FLEES
BECAUSE SHE DOESN'T KNOW
HOW TO SCREAM.

It will be difficult
to find her.

I OPEN THE DRAWER
AND FEEL FOR
THE FLASHLIGHT.

I FIND THUMBTACKS,
COINS, PILLS,
AND BREADCRUMBS.

Loose bobby pins,
rubber bands,
staplers,
and [staples].

TRANSPARENT

ADHESIVE TAPE.

TRANSPARENT
ADHESIVE TAPE.

BUSINESS CARDS

★   ★

TOBACCO AND RICE PAPER.

MATCHES, A CANDLE.

THE FLASHLIGHT.

I CALL OUT TO THE DEAF GIRL,
BUT SHE DOESN'T ANSWER.

I LIGHT UP THE HALLWAY:
SHE'S NOT THERE.

"FOLLOW HER," YELLS
THE LAME MAN. "RUN!"

THE ONE-ARMED MAN
THUMPS THE DIVIDING SCREENS
THAT SEPARATE
OUR WORKSTATIONS.

THE CLOCK FALLS TO THE FLOOR.

12 : 12 PM

THE PERSONNEL ARE RESTLESS.

THE CAGES ARE OPENED

PROCEED

THE DOGS ARE RELEASED.

It's the howling
of a pack of hounds
before
the violence begins.

THE ONE-EYED MAN REMEMBERS,
SCREAMS: HE SEES THEM COMING.

THE BLIND GIRL KEEPS
STILL WHILE THE
DOGS SNIFF AT HER.

She's in heat.

THE SOUNDS IN THE STREET
COPULATE
WITH OURS.

THE DEAF GIRL YELLS OUT
WITH AUTHORITY:
"SILENCE!
WHERE IS THE MUTE GIRL!"

SILENCE.

ABSENT.

INDIVIDUAL FINGERPRINT

Serial

Sec.

Right Thumbprint

NOTIFIED

THE SUBSIDIARY

☎ 4 755 6320

SALVADOR PIEDRAS S/N

07 JUN 2008

I LIGHT UP MY DESK
AND SEE PENDING INSTRUCTIONS:

THE OUTAGE WILL BE EXTENDED
INDEFINITELY.

Access
WILL REMAIN CLOSED
UNTIL SERVICES ARE RESTORED

DUE TO CIRCUMSTANCES
BEYOND OUR CONTROL.

ALL PERSONNEL SHALL COMPLY
UNTIL FURTHER NOTICE.

08 JUN 2008

THE LAME MAN
HOLDS A BOY CAPTIVE
AND TEACHES HIM TO READ.

THE MUTE GIRL TOLD ME THIS
WHEN SHE CAME TO ME
FOR PILLS.

I SHINED THE LIGHT IN HER EYES.
THEY TURNED GRAY.

THE MUTE GIRL DIDN'T BLINK.

I OPENED THE DRAWER,
RELUCTANTLY.

A FINE CUT:
THE SONG OF A SHEET
OF PAPER.

I DROPPED THE FLASHLIGHT.

THE MUTE GIRL BENT DOWN
SLOWLY AND LEFT IT SWITCHED OFF
ON TOP OF MY DESK.

I FELT IT...

She approached in the dark.
She licked up the blood.

"It stings," I told her.
"Your teeth are hurting me."

THE MUTE GIRL WENT ON CALMLY
AND IN DETAIL.

THE BOY WAS LOST.

HE WAS POOR, WITHOUT MANNERS:
THE LAME MAN
HAD TO BATHE HIM.

THE MUTE GIRL SHOWED ME
HOW HE DID IT.

EXPERTLY, UNTIL
HE GREW BIG.

He surrounded the darkness
with fingerprints.

AND IT LEFT HIM DRY.

That's how the story ended
and the rumor began.

THE MUTE GIRL SMOOTHED
HER SKIRT AND DISAPPEARED
AT THE SAME TIME.

WITHOUT SAYING A WORD.

STAINED.

COD.263// ANALOGICAL
        OFFICE
        ARTICLES

The blind girl said:
    "All negligence
is deliberate."

THE MUTE GIRL
STOLE MY RED INK.

I DIDN'T REALIZE.

(I LET IT HAPPEN.)

QUALIFIES
FOR
POSITION

The lame man said:
"Life itself
is a worthy career."

I USED TO WORK
IN A BANK.

My SKILLS ARE MANUAL.

I USED TO BE A TELLER IN A BRANCH.

WINDOW
1 4

NON-ACCOUNT HOLDING
CLIENTS

RECEIVED
CANCELED
REVISED
DISPATCHED

GUARANTEED

---

4 DEC 7 NOV 8 OCT 4 DEC 7 NOV 8 OCT
11 SEP 16 AUG 17 JUL 11 SEP 16 AUG 17 JUL
18 JUN 20 MAY 28 APR 18 JUN 20 MAY 28 APR
25 MAR 28 FEB 30 JAN 25 MAR 28 FEB 30 JAN
4 DEC 7 NOV 8 OCT 4 DEC 7 NOV 8 OCT
11 SEP 16 AUG 17 JUL 11 SEP 16 AUG 17 JUL
18 JUN 20 MAY 28 APR 18 JUN 20 MAY 28 APR
25 MAR 28 FEB 30 JAN 25 MAR 28 FEB 30 JAN
4 DEC 7 NOV 8 OCT 4 DEC 7 NOV 8 OCT
11 SEP 16 AUG 17 JUL 11 SEP 16 AUG 17 JUL
18 JUN 20 MAY 28 APR 18 JUN 20 MAY 28 APR
25 MAR 28 FEB 30 JAN 25 MAR 28 FEB 30 JAN
4 DEC 7 NOV 8 OCT 4 DEC 7 NOV 8 OCT
11 SEP 16 AUG 17 JUL 11 SEP 16 AUG 17 JUL
18 JUN 20 MAY 28 APR 18 JUN 20 MAY 28 APR
25 MAR 28 FEB 30 JAN 25 MAR 28 FEB 30 JAN
4 DEC 7 NOV 8 OCT 4 DEC 7 NOV 8 OCT
11 SEP 16 AUG 17 JUL 11 SEP 16 AUG 17 JUL
18 JUN 20 MAY 28 APR 18 JUN 20 MAY 28 APR
25 MAR 28 FEB 30 JAN 25 MAR 28 FEB 30 JAN

APPROVED
TO PAY

INITIALS   DATE

They didn't fire me,
one afternoon I left.

I WALKED OUT OF THE BRANCH
DURING MY LUNCH BREAK.

→

I WASN'T HUNGRY.

I WALKED.

I COVERED DISTANCES
THAT SEEMED GREAT.

I VISITED:

1	CIRCUS
1	PRISON
+ | 2 | HOSPITAL |

---

4 | MENTAL
FACILITIES

THEY CONTACTED ME
FOR MY MEDICAL RECORDS.

RETINAL ACHROMATOPSIA:
I'M COLOR-BLIND.

I WAS THE LAST ONE
TO FIND OUT.

I ACCEPTED THE TESTS.

THEY CUT OFF MY HAIR.

They fixed electrodes
to my shaved parts.

Don't fall asleep, she told me.'

THE NURSE
TOUCHED MY CHEST
WITH HER COLD HAND.

THE VOLTAGE OSCILLATES.

The resistances burn
until the fuses
blow.

1 SHORT-CIRCUIT

1 ELECTROSHOCK

IT SMELLS LIKE
FISH SCALES.

It's the melted plastic
of the wall sockets.

THE SILENCE
OF THE GENERATOR.

THE CUT LINES.

AT THE SUBSIDIARY
THEY USE THE CABLES
FOR OTHER THINGS.

To be safe,
they went back
to seals
and rubber stamps.

So that the information can exist.

SO IT CAN BE
RECORDED

It's beside the point.

I STAMP THE ORDERS,
THE INSTRUCTIONS,
THE MANDATES.

THESE ARE MY
FINGERPRINTS.

13 JUN 2008

THE ONE-ARMED MAN RETURNS
MY INK.

HE SWELLS WITH PRIDE
AT HIS HEROIC DEED.

His stump served
as a coat hook,

WHEN
THE BLIND GIRL REMOVED
HER COAT.

16 JUN 2008

"The lame man is a fag."

THAT'S WHAT THE ONE-ARMED MAN
WROTE WHILE WE
WAITED FOR HER   WC
IN THE BATHROOM.

I'M AT THE REAR, WITH
THE FLASHLIGHT: I THINK
ABOUT THE BOY HE
KEEPS CAPTIVE.

THE BLIND GIRL ENTERS
AND STOPS
IN FRONT OF THE MIRROR:
SHE KNOWS SHE IS BEING OBSERVED.

LIKE A SHIVER,
THE DOOR OPENS.
THE MUTE GIRL
ENTERS AND HIDES HERSELF.

My light in the reflection
reveals them together.

THE BLIND GIRL
BELIEVES SHE IS TOUCHING HERSELF.

THE MUTE GIRL, TO HER EAR,
TELLS HER NO.

THERE ARE FOUR OF US
IN A NARROW BATHROOM.

CONDENSATION COVERS THE DOOR,
THE MIRROR,
THE WALLS.

Dogs can be heard barking.

They scrape at the door
with their teeth.

"THEY'RE ON THE LOOSE!"
SCREAMS THE ONE-EYED MAN
FROM OUTSIDE.

THE LAME MAN ENTERS
BY FORCE,
KICKING IN THE DOOR.

THE DOGS CORNER
THE FEMALES: THE ONE-EYED MAN
LAUNCHES HIMSELF FORWARD TO PROTECT THEM.

The mute girl moans.
The one-armed man applauds.
The blind girl cries.

IT IS IMPOSSIBLE TO TELL APART
THE ANIMALS.

17 JUN 2008

A FLY
CIRCLES THE BODY
OF THE BLIND GIRL.

They carry her off
without a shroud:
she died naked.

THE DEAF GIRL ASKS ME:
"AREN'T THERE ANY CANDLES?"

She brings in
a pending order.

THEY'RE LOOKING FOR ANOTHER PERSON.

ANOTHER WOMAN.

"SAVE HER," SHE SAYS TO ME.

BSIDIARY

1. THE ACTION PROCEEDS
   DUE TO SUSPICIO

CANCELED

18 JUN 2008

IN THE COMING HOURS,

To all personnel.

WE ANNOUNCE   █ █

SERVICES ARE   █ █

RESTORED.

   THE SUBSIDIARY

19 : 53 P M

THE DIVIDING SCREENS
SEPARATING
THE CUBICLES.

THE HALLWAYS
STAINED
WITH BLOOD.

A FRACTION
OF A SECOND:

THE CURRENT SHAKES THE BUILDING.
A MEDIUM-INTENSITY TREMOR. THE
DISCHARGE INCREASES PROGRESSIVELY,
CONTROLLED. JUST THE SOUND OF THE
GENERATOR, A REAL BUZZING, ALMOST
IMMINENT, INTENSIFYING
UNTIL THE DOGS ARE DEAFENED. IT SEEMS
IMPERCEPTIBLE. IT BURNS. THE LIGHTS
GO ON SUDDENLY, BLINDING OUR EYES.
THE LIGHT REVEALS EVERYONE IN THEIR PLACES.

CIVIL COURT
OF THE 6TH CIRCUIT

18.06.08

SECRETARY
SANTIAGO

I HAD ACCESS TO THE REPORTS.

I saw the photographs.

My reaction was adverse.

ROUTINE – YEARS GO BY – PERSIST.

THE PERSONNEL
INDIFFERENT
AT THEIR RESPECTIVE
WORKSTATIONS.

The Subsidiary was written and produced using Trodat 4253, 4912, 4954, and M450 stamps, with three- and four-millimeter movable type on plates displaying four to six lines of text and a maximum of ninety characters per impression. This work forms part of a collection of eight different objects found at an employee's workstation, and was printed by the author in collaboration with Obrera Gráfica. One of these works constitutes the holotype Notarial foliado, stamped on pages measuring 24 by 35.5 centimeters, as reproduced in this edition.

MATÍAS CELEDÓN was born in Santiago, Chile, in 1981. He is a screenwriter, a journalist, and the author of three novels.

SAMUEL RUTTER is a writer and translator from Melbourne, Australia.